QUOTES, JOKES and STORIES TO LIVE BY
Mostly from the "Hood"

Quotes, Jokes and Stories To Live By: Mostly from the Hood
Copyright © 2023 by Frederick Jordan

Published in the United States of America

Library of Congress Control Number: 2024915887
ISBN   Paperback: 979-8-89091-181-0
ISBN   eBook: 979-8-89091-182-7

All rights reserved. No part of this publication may be reproduced, stored in a retrieval system or transmitted in any way by any means, electronic, mechanical, photocopy, recording or otherwise without the prior permission of the author except as provided by USA copyright law.

The opinions expressed by the author are not necessarily those of ReadersMagnet, LLC.

ReadersMagnet, LLC
10620 Treena Street, Suite 230 | San Diego, California, 92131 USA
1. 619. 354. 2643 | www.readersmagnet.com

Book design copyright © 2023 by ReadersMagnet, LLC. All rights reserved.

Cover design by Ericka Obando
Interior design by Daniel Lopez

QUOTES, JOKES and STORIES TO LIVE BY
Mostly from the "Hood"

FREDERICK JORDAN

ReadersMagnet, LLC

FOREWORD

By

Frederick Jordan

Writing this was truly a joy. If you love what you are doing, you will never work a day of your life. I never learned so much and laughed so long recalling the advice and counsel on life from everyday people.

This book, "Quotes, Jokes, and Stories to Live By," is meant to be a guide to enhance one's life and to facilitate the critical decisions that one continually faces. It is a "no nonsense," down to earth advice and counsel from not only scholars and famous people, but mostly from ordinary people surviving in the ghetto or low income neighborhoods, commonly known as the "HOOD."

The quotes in this book are not necessarily referenced by me or the original author, but by the person I heard it from. Of course most of the stories can't be verified as true because they originated from the barbershops, drinking establishments, or Saturday night parties. However, the stories are important because they serve as a "hint and a half" or real time lesson for one who must be continually aware of the challenges of life.

QUOTES, JOKES, AND STORIES TO LIVE BY

(Mostly from the "Hood")
By
Frederick Jordan

ON ACHIEVEMENT - *Quotes*

- In order to have what you never had; you must do what you have never done.
  - *Frederick Jordan*

- We do what we have to do; so we can do what we want to do.
  - *Nannette Cutliff, Walnut Creek*

ON ADVANTAGE - *Quotes*

- We gain the advantage in any situation through one medium: TIME. We gain the advantage by doing things before they need to be done-positioning ourselves ahead of time in the best place. Those who think ahead of the approaching action will have the advantage. They will be the winners.
  - *Wynn Davis, Author, The Best of Success*

- When everyone is out partying or sleeping tight, I am working upwards through the night. The next day, at the rising sun, my work has already begun……….. The winner's edge.
  - *Frederick Jordan*

ON ADVANTAGE - *Story*

- Geese take advantage of flying and working together as a team. As each goose flaps its wings, it creates "uplift" for the bird following. By flying in a "V" formation, the whole flock adds 71% flyer range than if each bird flew alone. When the lead goose gets tired, it rotates back into the formation and another goose flies at the point position. When a goose gets sick, wounded, or shot down, two geese drop out of formation and follow it down to help and protect it. They stay with the goose until it is either able to fly again or dies. Then they launch out on their own formation or catch up with the flock. The geese in formation honk from behind to encourage those up front to keep up their speed.
  - *Internet*

ON AFFIRMATIVE ACTION - *Quotes*

- First it was about civil rights, then about affirmative action… Now it is time for silver rights.
  - *Southside, Chicago*

- Affirmative Action is the most conservative, the most modest, the most miniscule response to a horrific history that we've had.
  - *Charles Ogletree, Professor, Harvard Law School, 2003*

- Affirmative Action is not the most America can do for us. Frankly, it is the least America can do for us.
  - *Dr. Julianne Malveaux, Economist and Syndicated Columnist*

ON AFRICA - *Quotes*

> Aids attacks the body
> Discrimination attacks the spirit
> Aids is caused by a virus
> Discrimination is caused by ignorance
> Avoid being infected by either one
> - *Sign on office building, Accra, Ghana*

- Not everyone who chased the zebra, caught it; but the one who caught it, chased it.
  - *African Proverb from S'mangaliso, South Africa*

ON AGE

- Age is about mind over matter: If you don't mind, then it doesn't matter.
  - *Satchel Page, age 53, Oldest Professional Baseball Player*

- You are not old when your hair turns gray
  You are not old when your teeth decay
  But when your mind makes a date
  That your body can't take
  That's when you are old!
  - *Jack McKnight, Sacramento, CA*

- You are only as old as you *FEEL*, as you *LOOK*, and most important, as you *THINK!*
Don't fall for that chronology psychology!
- Frederick Jordan, San Francisco

- Age is nothing but a number, and my number is unlisted!
- Jack McKnight, Sacramento, CA

- A man who correctly guesses a woman's age may be smart, but he is not very bright.
- From the Hood

- We don't stop playing because we are growing old. We grow old because we stop playing.
- George Bernard Shaw

- A woman is allowed to lie about two things: how old she is and how many boyfriends she has had.
- Frederick Jordan

- It's better to hang out with people better than you. Pick out associates whose behavior is better than yours and you'll drift to that direction.
- Warren Buffett, Billionaire

- There comes a point in your life when you realize:
Who matter,
Who never did,
Who won't anymore,
And who always will.

So, don't worry about people from your past.
There's a reason why they didn't make it to your future.
GIVE FLOWERS TO EVERYONE YOU DON'T WANT TO LOSE
- *Internet*

ON ATTITUDE - *Quotes*

- You're hell when you're well…but you stay sick half the time.
  - *From the "Hood"*

- Your gratitude should be your attitude!
  - *Frederick Jordan, San Francisco*

- Everyone wants the best things in life, but not everyone wants to put up with the toil and strife.
  - *Bobby Womack, Singer*

- If life knocks you down, try to land on your back because if you can look up, you can get up.
  - *Larry Ivory, Peoria, Illinois*

- Strive to get to the top because the bottom is over-crowded.
  - *From the "Hood"*

- I would rather attempt to do something and fail than to do nothing and succeed.
  - *Larry Ivory, Peoria, Illinois*

- If it ain't broke, don't fix it.
  - *From the Hood*

ON BUSINESS - *Quotes*

- Business is politics and politics is business.
  - Frederick Jordan

- In business, if you do not plan to succeed, then PLAN TO FAIL
  - Frederick Jordan

- You do not go into business with one who has nothing to lose.... But you do.
  - Frederick Jordan

- If you plan to go somewhere in business...
  You need to look like you are already there
  - Frederick Jordan

- You should dress to impress
  Then do the rest,
  To look and be the best.
  - Frederick Jordan

ON BUSINESS - *Story*

- Business Plan Story - The story is that when the flamboyant, well-dressed, former San Francisco Mayor Willie Brown was Speaker of the California State Assembly, he had a reception at a popular San Francisco nightclub called MUMMS owned by Gene Washington, Wide Receiver of the San Francisco 49er's. One of the attendees, visiting from Idaho, was admiring his alligator shoes and wanted to know where he could find alligators to get into the alligator shoe business.

Brown responded, with a questionable look, that he could find alligators in the Everglades of Florida. Another person overhearing the conversation, commented, "You better get a business plan." The next day, the Idaho visitor takes a plane to Florida, rents a boat, and proceeds into the Everglades. He immediately comes upon this big ole alligator and jumps into the water to capture him. After a fierce battle, with blood everywhere, he pulls the alligator up on the riverbank, turns him over on his back, and disappointingly exclaims, "Just my luck, this alligator is barefoot!"

.........Then kicks the alligator back into the water!

(Stanford Alumni Tracy Webb: no Business Plan, no Market Research, and then kicked his assets back into the water).
- *Frederick Jordan*

- Business Partner Story - Two men went into business together. One had the money and the other had the expertise. After two years, they broke up. The one who had the money parted with the expertise. The one with the expertise parted with the money…and his expertise.
  - *Vice President, Wells Fargo Bank*

- Business goes on - The Pope and Colonel Sanders - Long time ago, there was this young black guy who lived in Harlem and was known to be able to sell anything. He was negotiating on selling the Brooklyn Bridge. Colonel Sanders of the Chicken chain sent for him with the task of sending him to the Pope to sell an innovative idea to the Pope. The presentation was that if he could convince the Pope to change the Our Father prayer to say, "Give us this day our daily chicken" instead of "Give us this day our daily bread," there would be $300 million placed in the Vatican account.

The next day, the young man flew to Rome and met with the Pope at their arranged meeting. The Pope responded, "No, no, no! It has been like this for over 2,000 years." The young man responded that he was authorized to raise the donation to $400 million and to please give serious consideration.

Two days later, the Pope called all the Cardinals to an urgent meeting. "Fathers, I have good news and bad news." He continued, "The good news is that today, we have $400 million donated to the Vatican Account." He then continued, "The bad news is that we lost the Wonder Bread Account."
- *The Hood*

ON CHARACTER - *Quotes*

- "Judge a man, not by the color of his skin, but by the content of his character."
  - *Dr. Martin Luther King, Jr.*

- It was character that got us out of bed, commitment that moved us into action, and discipline that enabled us to follow through.
  - *Zip Ziglar*

- No matter how you feel, get up, dress up, and show up.
  - *Internet*

- You have to decide who you are and force the world to deal with you, not with its idea of you.
  - *James Baldwin*

- It is difficulties that show what men are.
  - *Unknown*

ON CHARACTER - *Story*

- Late in the Vietnam War, I was drafted and graduated from Officers Training School in Texas. As an African American driving back to the East Coast after graduation, with three white fellow graduates, in our new 2nd Lt. Blues, I had a flat tire on a highway outside of Tuscaloosa, Alabama. Seeking help on the side of the road, we were refused assistance by some white drivers because we were racially mixed. Furthermore, we almost got run over by another white driver for the same reason.

I learned later that a black woman also had a flat in the rain on the same highway. Drivers, white and black, passed her when finally, a white driver stopped. He took her to the nearest gas station to dry, returned and fixed the tire, brought her back to her car, and sent her on her way. A few days later, the man received a huge bouquet of flowers with a note stating how much she appreciated his assistance at such a time of sorrow in her life. She was on her way to bury her husband.
- *Signed Mrs. Nat King Cole*
- *Lieutenant Frederick Jordan*

ON CIVIL RIGHTS

- In the old days we demanded "CIVIL RIGHTS." Today, we demand "SILVER RIGHTS!"
  - *From the "Hood"*

- If you are neutral in situations of injustice, you have chosen the side of the oppressor.
  - *Archbishop Desmond Tutu, South Africa*

- Those who deny freedom to others deserve it not for themselves, and, under a just God, cannot long retain it.
  - *Abraham Lincoln*

ON COMMUNICATION - *Quotes*

- Do not kill the "message," because of the "messenger."
  - *Dale Dawson, Walnut Creek, CA*

ON DESTINY - *Quotes*

- Life has choices: You can hang around the mud puddles where the tadpoles stay… or you can go out to sea where the big fish play.
  - *Frederick Jordan*

- Make your destiny a matter of choice, not a matter of chance.
  - *From the "Hood"*

- It doesn't matter what he does, he will never amount to anything.
  - *Albert Einstein's Teacher, 1885*

- For every happening there's a reason.
  - *Sharon Blanco, San Francisco, California*

- Those who cannot remember the past are condemned to repeat it.
  - *George Santayana*

- The belief is that God has a plan for everyone in life. This plan is communicated through destinies and coincidences. If you keep ignoring these signals, then you may be ignoring the plan that God has for you.
  - *Frederick Jordan*

- The Essence of Destiny:
  Watch your thoughts for they become words; Chose your words for they become actions; Understand your actions for they become habits; Study your habits, for they will become your character. Develop your character, for it becomes your destiny.
  - *Frank Outlaw*

ON DECEPTION - *Quotes*

- I was born at night, but not last night.
  - *From the "Hood"*

- Deception is a strategy in the art of war.
  - *General Sen Tsu, The Art of War*

- I'm not fattening frogs......for **snakes.**

ON DECEPTION - *Story*

- A mother decided to visit her college freshman son to check up on him. On arrival, he announced that he had a fellow female student housemate. After a couple of days, the mother asked her son if there was anything romantic between him and his roommate. The son vehemently denied any involvement.

A week after the mother's return, the housemate complained that her ladle had been missing since his mother had left. So the son wrote his mother, "I'm not saying you did, and I am not saying you didn't, but since you have been gone, my housemate's ladle has been missing." Two days later, the mother wrote back to her son, "I'm not saying that you did, and I am not saying that you didn't, but if your housemate was sleeping in her own bed, she would have found her ladle."
- I forgot who told me this!

ON EDUCATION - *Quotes*

- Education is our passport to the future, for tomorrow belongs to the people who prepare for it today.
  - Malcolm X, Black Muslim and Civil Rights Leader

- Education is expensive, but ignorance is more expensive.
  - Julius Maada Bio, President of Sierra Leone

- One can best prepare themselves for the economic future by investing in their own education. If you study hard and learn at a young age, you will be in the best circumstances to secure your future.
  - Warren Buffett, Billionaire

- Give a man a fish and you feed him for a day. Teach a man how to fish and you feed him for a lifetime.
  - *Chinese Proverb*

- Knowledge is knowing what to do next; virtue is doing it.
  - *David Starr Jordan*

- A Mind is a Terrible Thing to Waste
  - *Dr. Arthur Fletcher, United Negro College Fund, Father of Affirmative Action*

ON EMPLOYMENT - *Quotes*

- Three reasons to hire an older woman-they don't tell; they don't swell; and they're grateful as hell.
  - *Joe Oakley, Richmond, CA*

- A good secretary says, "Good morning, sir." A nice secretary says, "It's morning, sir."
  - *Ying Zhang, Alamo, CA and Shanghai, China*

- I don't get my "honey" where I make my "money."
  - *From the "Hood"*

- The graveyards of the world are filled with indispensable people.
  - *Frank Devlin, PE, Program Manager, Oakland, CA*

- The difference between unemployment in the White and Black population is like… when white people have a cold, then the black community has pneumonia.
  - *From the "Hood"*

- The closest to perfection a person ever comes is when he fills out a job application.
  - *Stanley J. Randal*

- Pick a job that you love, and you will never work a day in your life.
  - *Timothy Simon, Securities Attorney, San Francisco*

- Hire people smarter than you are and get out of their way.
  - *Successful Business Practice*

- Before you have an argument with your boss, take a good look at both sides-his side and the outside.
  - *Stanley J. Randall*

ON ECONOMIC STATUS - *Quotes*

- You can only attain the status of Middle Class by working a job. To attain the status of Wealth, you must go into business or make investments.
  - *Frederick Jordan*

THE FIVE ECONOMIC STATES OF URBAN LIFE:

- The Arrival and Survival - concerned with basic food and shelter to support life.

- The Struggle and the Juggle - "Robbing Peter to pay Paul."
- Sustaining and Maintaining - "Meeting the basic requirements of family life."
- Railing and Sailing - "The middle class doing well with BMW in garage, vacations, and country home."
- Roaring and Soaring - "The upper class with major business holdings, residential estate or ranch, vacations, and vacation homes."

  - Black University of Southern California Professor, South Central, LA

ON FINANCIAL - *Quotes*

- If you want to be bullish, as in the Stock Market, you need to run with the bulls.

  - Frederick Jordan

- Live below your means and invest the rest. You will not become rich by saving, but by investing.

  - George Fraser, Speaker/Author

ON FINANCIAL - *Story*

- One time, a 91-year-old man and an 89-year-old woman came into this psychiatrist's office and asked him to observe them while they had sex. Afterwards, the doctor astonished, remarked, "That was remarkable," and charged them $32. The next week the couple came back and requested the same, and paid $32. After two more return trips, the psychiatrist said, "Why do you continue to come back? You are great!" The elderly gentlemen spoke up, "Well, Doctor, the little lady over there is married and I live in a retirement home. The

Hilton is $120 a night and Holiday Inn is $89. We can come here for $32, get a receipt to send to Medicare, and get $28 back, costing us $4.00."
- *John Tolson, Suitland, MD*

ON FREEDOM - *Quotes*

- Freedom is not something that one people can bestow on another as a gift. They claim it as their own and none can keep it from them
  - *Kwame Nkrumah, first President of Ghana, leading it to independence in 1957*

- My humanity is bound up in yours, for we can only be human together.
  - *Desmond Tutu, South African Archbishop known for his work against apartheid and human rights*

- I had reasoned this out in my mind; there was one of two things I had a right to, liberty, or death; if I could not have one, I would have the other; for no man should take me alive.
  - *Harriet Tubman, Abolitionist and made famous the Underground Railroad for slaves.*

ON FRUSTRATION - *Quotes*

- You can't make a purse out of a pig's ear.
  - *Fred Jordan's Grandfather, John Frederick, St. Mary's County, MD*

- You just can't shine sh*t.
  - *Lyndon Baines Johnson, former US President*

ON GENERATIONS

- A people without knowledge of their past history, origin, and culture are like a tree without roots.
  - *Marcus Garvey, Emancipator*

- The founder of Dubai, Sheikh Rashid, wondered about the future of his country, and he said: "My grandfather rode a camel; my father rode a camel and I drove a Mercedes; my son drives a Land Rover and my grandson is going to drive a Land Rover; but my great grandson is going to have to walk the camel again …"

  Why?

  "Difficult times create strong people; strong people create easy times. Easy times create weak people, weak people create difficult times."

  Many will not understand, but you must create warriors.

  The same is when you give everything for free to your child who sleeps all day.
  - *Elena Restituyo, La Vega, Dominican Republic*

ON GREATNESS

- Awareness of impermanence is encouraged so that when it is coupled with our appreciation of the enormous potential of

our human existence, it will give us a sense of urgency that one must use every precious moment.
- *The 14th Dalai Lama*

ON HEALTH - *Quotes*

- Your health is a matter of daily management. If you don't manage it every day, it will manage you in some way.
  - *Frederick E. Jordan*

- Growing old beats the alternative of dying young.
  - *From the "Hood"*

ON HAPPINESS

- Happiness can be found, even in the darkest of time, if one only remembers to turn on the light.
  - *Albus Dumbledore*

- If you want others to be happy, practice compassion. If you want to be happy, practice compassion.
  - *Dalai Lama*

- There are shortcuts to happiness, and dancing is one of them.
  - *Vicki Baum*

ON HONESTY - *Quotes*

- To every bit of jest, there is some truth.
  - *Nur Abby Hussein, Mogadishu, Somalia*

ON IMAGINATION - *Quotes*

- Never be limited by other people's limited imagination.
  - *Mae Jemison, NASA Astronaut, and first Black woman in space*

- Nothing is impossible. With so many people saying it couldn't be done, all it takes is imagination.
  - *Michael Phelps, U. S. Swimming, Olympics*

- Don't let anyone rob you of your imagination, your creativity, or your curiosity. It's your place in the world: It's your life. Go on and do all you can with it and make it the life you want to live.
  - *Dr. Mae Jamison, NASA Astronaut*

ON JOSELING IN THE "HOOD"

- A GREETING:
  What's the word? Response: "Thunderbird!" (A cheap wine)
  What's the price? Response: "Thirty Twice" (60 cents)
  What's the reason? Response: "Grapes out of season."
  (Today it's "Two Buck Chuck," Charles Shaw Wines Trader Vic's for $2
  - *From the "Hood"*

- A CHALLENGE:
  I'll tell you what I got for you...... A dirty look! A left hook! Your body shook! Your money took! And your name on the "Sick Book!"
  - *Lewis Jordan, Washington, DC*

- NO CONTEST:
  My name is Bob Jones…………..skin and bones
  I'm too light to fight……… and (if so) too thin to win.
  ……. Bob Jones, KBLX Radio Station, San Francisco

ON JUSTICE - *Quotes*

- If you are neutral in situations of injustice, you have chosen the side of the oppressor.
  - Archbishop Desmond Tutu, South Africa

- Those in the pursuit of justice do not fear the consequences.
  - Frederick Jordan

- For many in the status quo, Justice means "Just - us!"
  - Los Angeles Riots, 1965

ON JUSTICE - *Story*

- POLITICAL JUSTICE - When Joe Califano, Jr., former US Secretary of Health, Education, and Welfare (HEW) was under criticism by opposing US Congressional Representatives, he had the following to say: "Those who attack me are supposed to attack me based on evidence. If they have no evidence, then they attack based on circumstances, known as circumstantial evidence. If they have neither, than they attack me personally. When I am attacked personally, then I know that my opponents don't have a leg to stand on!"
  - Frederick Jordan

ON LABOR - *Story*

- TOIL IS MEANINGLESS - So my heart began to despair over all my toilsome labor under the sun. For a man may do his work with wisdom, knowledge, and skill, and then he must leave all he owns to someone who has not worked for it. This, too, is meaningless and a great misfortune.

  What does a man get for all the toil and anxious striving with which he labors under the sun? All his days of work are pain and grief; even at night his mind does not rest. This, too, is meaningless.

  A man can do nothing better than to eat and drink and find satisfaction in his work.
  - Ecclesiastes 2:17 - 25

ON LEADERSHIP - *Quotes*

- History's greatest leader, who changed the whole world, had only 12 followers... and one of them was "shaky."
  - From the "Hood"

- Leadership is generally defined as the capacity to make things happen that would otherwise not happen.
  - Thomas E. Cronin

- THE GOLDEN RULE - He, who has the gold, makes the rule.
  - From the "Hood"

- He, who shakes the apple tree, rarely gets an apple.
  - *From the "Hood"*

- My dad says the early bird gets the worm, but my granddad says the second mouse gets the cheese.
  - *Ebony Magazine, August 2002*

ON LEADERSHIP - *Story*

- Rank has its privileges: Charley, a new retiree-account manager, just couldn't seem to get to work on time. Every day he was 5, 10, 15 minutes late. But he was a good worker, really tidy, clean-shaven, sharp-minded, and a real credit to the company.

  One day, the boss called him into the office for a talk. "Charley, I have to tell you, I like your work, you do a bang-up job, but your being late so often is quite bothersome."

  "Yes, I know boss, and I am working on it."
  "Well good, you are a team player. That's what I like to hear"
  "It's odd though, you're coming in late. I know you are retired from the Armed Forces, what did they say if you came in late there?"

  They said, "Good morning, Admiral, can I get your coffee, Sir."
  - *US Military Officer*

ON LOVE - *Quotes*

- If you can't be with the one you love, then love the one you're with.
  - Aretha Franklin

- If you don't want my love, don't knock it. There are plenty of others who would love to rock it.
  - Wilson Pickett, Singer, and Writer

- One man's trash is another man's treasure.
  - From the "Hood"

- Romance, without finance, ain't got a chance.
  - From the "Hood"

- Love does not consist in gazing at each other, but in looking outward together in the same direction.
  - Antoine de Saint-Exupery

- Love recognizes no barriers. It jumps hurdles, leaps fences, penetrates walls to arrive at its destination full of hope
  - Unknown

- Jealousy in romance is like salt in food. A little can enhance the savor, but too much can spoil the pleasure and, under certain circumstances, can be life-threatening.
  - Unknown

ON LOVE - *Jokes*

- Women are like apples on the tree. The best ones are at the top of the tree. Most men don't want to reach for the good ones because they are afraid of falling and getting hurt. Instead, they just get the rotten apples from the ground that aren't as good, but easy.

  So, the apples at the top think something is wrong with them, when in reality, they're amazing. They just have to wait for the right man to come along, the one who's brave enough to climb all the way to the top of the tree.

And.... men are like fine wine. They start out as grapes, and it's up to women to stomp the crap out of them until they turn into something acceptable.... to have dinner with.
  - *Dale Dawson, Walnut Creek, CA*

ON MARRIAGE - *Quotes*

- Why buy the cow when the milk is free.
  - *From the "Hood"*

- Marriage is a 3-ring process:
  1. Engagement ring
  2. Wedding Ring
  3. Suffering
  - *Unknown*

- You will never really get to know someone, until you live together under the same roof.
  - *Maria Cuaresma's mother, Quezon City, Philippines*

ON MODERATION - *Story and Joke*

- A bunch of old guys would sit around playing chess in the park all day. One day, a new guy showed up. He was pretty wrinkled and had white hair and he got in a game with one of the old guys. After looking at the guy for a while, he said "You know, I just noticed: You are not wearing glasses, you got your real teeth, you got no hearing aid, and you look like you are in pretty good shape."

The new guy said, "Well, when I was a kid, my parents took me to the doctor because I stayed in the house, reading books and not getting exercise. The doctor said that if I wanted to stay in shape, I should make love with a woman four times a day. So that is what I have been doing to this very day."
"Really, how old are you?"
"Twenty-four."
- *Jan Murray, The Friars Club*

ON MARRIAGE - *Joke*

- Two people got married. But the husband was a little lazy. Shortly after their marriage, he came home from work and his wife exclaimed, "Honey, you took my new car and left me your old car and now it's broken." He responded, "Do I look like Henry Ford?" and went into the room and read his paper. The next day, he came home, and she met him, "You wouldn't let me buy a new washing machine and now the old one is broken." He responded, "Do I look like Mr. Maytag?" and sat down to read his paper. The next day he came home, and everything was working. "Who fixed everything?" he asked. "The man up the street," she responded. "How much did he charge?" "Well, he said I could either bake him a cake or have sex with him," she responded. "What kind of cake did you bake?" he asked. "Do I look like Betty Crocker?" she responded.

- From the "Hood"

- Three men from the "Hood" showed up at the gates of heaven at the same time. After verifying that they had not been involved in drugs or pimping, St. Peter said they could enter the pearly gates. But he had one question for each, "How many times did you cheat on your wife?" Since heaven was so large, St. Peter warned that the answer would determine the means of transportation to get around.

    The first man recalled about 12 times, but St. Peter corrected him to 32 times and assigned him a Volkswagen. The second man admitted to 10 times and got a Toyota. The third man recanted proudly that although he was a traveling salesman and his wife was sickly, he had never cheated on his wife. St. Peter assigned him a Cadillac El Dorado. However, after two days, the first two men passed the third man sitting on side of the road, crying next to his Cadillac. Puzzled, they asked, "You are in heaven, driving an El Dorado.... why would you be crying?" He answered, "I just saw my wife go by on a skateboard!"

    - Larry Ivory, Peoria, Illinois

ON MONEY - *Story*

- There was a guy named Leroy who went to the church every day, got on his knees, and asked, "Lord, please let me win the lottery. Lord, please, please let me win the lottery!" One day,

there was a loud thunderous noise, lightning and smoke, and a big voice responded, "Leroy, you have to help me……. You have to buy a ticket first."
- *From the "Hood"*

ON MONEY - *Quotes*

- For you women who spend all your money on clothes, be mindful that all your assets are on your ass.
  - *George Fraser, Speaker*

- He, who has the gold, is in control.
  - *From the "Hood"*

- He, who pays the piper, calls the tune.
  - *From the "Hood"*

- Some people say that money is the root of all evil. Wrong! It is NOT having money that is the root of all evil!
  - *Frederick Jordan*

ON MOVING ON - *Quotes*

- When one door closes, another opens, but we so often look so long and so regretfully upon the closed door, that we do not see the ones which open for us.
  - *Alexander Graham Bell*

- The truth is, unless you let go, unless you forgive yourself, unless you forgive the situation, unless you realize that the situation is over, you cannot move forward.
  - *Steve Maraboll*

- Every time you are tempted to react in the same old way, ask if you want to be a prisoner of the past or a pioneer of the future. The past is closed and limited; the future is open and free.
  - *Deepak Chopra*

- Mistakes are part of the game. It's how well you recover from them that's the mark of a great player.
  - *Alice Cooper*

ON NIGHT OWL - *Quotes*

- When I am completely myself, entirely alone or during the night when I cannot sleep, it is on such occasions that my ideas flow best and most abundantly. Whence and how these ideas come, I know not, nor can I force them.
  - *Wolfgang Amadeus Davis, Journalist and Writer*

- Whoever thinks about going to bed before twelve o'clock is a scoundrel.
  - *Samuel Johnson*

- No civilized person ever goes to bed the same day he gets up.
  - *Richard Harding, Journalist and Writer*

ON OPPORTUNITY - *Quotes*

- If while you are chasing that "pot of gold" at the end of what seems to be the rainbow and you fall into a diamond mine… become a miner.
  - *Frederick Jordan*

- Opportunity rarely comes at an opportune time. Carpe diem! (Seize the day.)
  - Frederick Jordan

- OPPORTUNITY COMES TO THOSE WHO:
  1. Have the Mind to Conceive it
  2. Have the Faith to Believe it
  3. Have the Commitment to Retrieve it
  4. Have the Preparation to Receive it
  - From the "Hood"

- If in doubt… DON'T.
  - Frederick E. Jordan

- To every misfortune, there is a good fortune…… Look for it.
  - Frederick Jordan

- Some men see things as they are and ask, "Why." I dream of things that never were and say, "why not."
  - Robert Kennedy, former US Presidential Candidate

- If opportunity knocks, let him in.
  Sit him down and become his friend.
  - Timothy Simon, Securities Attorney and CA State Commissioner

- Walls turned sideways are bridges.
  - Angela Davis, Black Panther Party

ON OPPORTUNITY - *Story*

- Once there was a flood and the water came up to the 1st floor level of John's house. A man in a rowboat came by and cried out, "John, better get into my boat." John replied, "I place my destiny in the hands of the Lord. I'll stay." When the water reached his second-floor bedroom, he replied the same to a neighbor in a speedboat. Later, while forced to withdraw to the roof, he turned down an offer to a helicopter, replying the same, "I place my destiny in the hands of the Lord, and I'll stay." Later, after he died, he asked St. Peter on approaching the gates of heaven, "St. Peter, I placed my destiny in the hands of the Lord, and look at me. I'm dead!" St. Peter responded, "Both the Lord and myself watched you down there in that flood. The Lord sent you a rowboat, a speedboat, and a helicopter. We shook our heads that you missed all of those opportunities after demonstrating such great faith. I guess you missed the boat."
  - *Frederick Jordan*

ON OPTIMISM AND PESSIMISM - *Quotes*

- Pessimists see the glass as half empty. Optimists see the glass as half full. Engineers see the glass twice as big as it ought to be.
  - *Civil Engineer, San Francisco*

- Pessimists are almost always wrong, and optimists are almost always right.
  - *Leslie Baker, Financial Services Round table, Nassau, Bahamas*

ON PHILOSOPHY ON LIFE - *Quotes*

- What matters is not wealth or status or power or fame, but how well we have loved…how we treat one another, that's entirely up to us.
  - President Barack Obama, Tucson Arizona victims Memorial service

- Sometimes it seems that… those who have the least ask for the most. And those for whom you do the most appreciate it the least.
  - Frederick Jordan

- Those who ask the most, give the least.
  - Frederick Jordan

- Get rid of those zeroes and find some heroes…with good sense.
  - Sherry Patton, Vallejo, CA

- Everything that "is" or "was," all started with a dream. Never stop DREAMING.
  - Yolanda Woodard

- Awareness of impermanence is encouraged so that when it is coupled with our appreciation of the enormous potential of our human existence, it will give us a sense of urgency that one must use every precious moment.
  - The 14th Dalai Lama

- Men may not get all they pay for in this world, but they must certainly pay for all they get.
  - *Frederick Douglass*

- Life is too short to have sorrow. You may be here today and gone tomorrow. You might as well get what you want. So go on and live, baby, go on and live.
  - *Neville Brothers in the song, "Tell it like it is"*

- Life is not measured by the number of breaths we take, but by the moments that take our breath away.
  - *Unknown*

- Life is not a journey to the grave with the intention of arriving safely in a pretty and well-preserved body, but rather to skid in sideways, champagne in one hand, strawberries in the other, body thoroughly used up, totally worn out, and loudly proclaiming - "WOW! What a ride!"
  - *Andre Jordan, Washington, DC*

- Work like you don't need the money. Dance like no one's watching you. Love like you've never been hurt!
  - *Store, Houston, TX Galleria Shopping Mall*

- God, give us grace to accept with serenity the things which cannot be changed, courage to change the things which should be changed, and the wisdom to distinguish one from the other.
  - *Reinhold Niebuhr*

ON PHILOSOPHY ON LIFE - *Jokes*

- Once there was a neighborhood dog that had an offspring that was no longer a puppy and ready to go into the world. So, he thought he would take him on a walk and give him some philosophy on life. While walking, they passed a meat store. He said, "Wait a minute, Son," and dashed across the street, grabbed a steak, and returned. They continued walking and talking and passed a female dog in heat. "Wait a minute, Son," and he dashed across the street, spent a little intimate time, and returned. They continued past a 7-11 store. "Wait a minute, Son," and he crossed the street, jumped up on the stool, bought a lottery ticket, and returned. They continued. Then they passed a fire hydrant. He dashed across the street, cocked his leg, and urinated on three sides. On returning, his son asked, "I didn't question the other things you did, but what was that ceremony about?" "Son, if it doesn't provide food, sex, or money, then piss on it!"
 - *From the "Hood"*

ON PHILANTHROPY - *Quotes*

- We make a living by what we get, but we make a life by what we give.
 - *Winston Churchill*

- If you give a man a fish, he will be back in a few days for more. If you teach him to fish, he may never have to return.
 - *Unknown*

ON PLANNING YOUR LIFE - *Quotes*

- If you do not PLAN to succeed, then PLAN to fail.
  - Unknown

- Those who cannot remember the past are condemned to repeat it.
  - George Santayana

- My mission in life is not merely to survive, but to thrive, and to do it with some passion, some compassion, some humor, and some style.
  - Unknown

ON RACE - *Story*

- Once there was a Zebra that went to the water pond every day and would stare at his own reflection in the water, wondering if he was white with black stripes or black with white stripes. Never finding out, he died and showed up at the pearly gates of heaven. Immediately, he asked St. Peter the question. St. Peter said go ask the Lord. Then come back and tell me what the Lord said.

  Later the Zebra returned and explained with frustration that the Lord said, "You are what you are!" "OK," responded St. Peter, "you are white with black stripes!" The Zebra, astounded, asks, "How did you know that?" "Oh if you were black, the Lord would have answered, 'You is, what it is!'"
  - From the "Hood"

ON REGRETS - *Quotes*

- I'd rather regret the risks that didn't work out than the chances I didn't take at all.
  - *Simone Biles*

- I don't believe in regret. I feel that everything leads us to where we are and we have to just jump forward, mean well, commit, and just see what happens.
  - *Angelina Jolie*

ON RELATIONSHIPS - *Quotes*

- You expect your friends to be with you through thick and thin. But when things get thick, the friends get thin.
  - *Marion Berry, former Mayor, Washington, DC January 9, 2000*

- Be careful of whose toes you step on today because they just may be connected to the ass you will have to kiss tomorrow.
  - *George Frazer, Author, <u>Success Runs in Our Race</u>*

- If you destroy a bridge, be sure you can swim.
  - *African Proverb*

- If you can't change the people around you... then change the people you are around.
  - *Barbara Rogers, KPIX News Anchor, San Francisco*

- My friendship is like a Rolls Royce. Everyone knows its value. Not everyone can afford the luxury of my friendship.
  - *Dr. Mera Horne, Mechanical Engineer, NASA*

- There comes a point in life when you realize:
  Who matters?
  Who never did?
  Who won't anymore…
  And who always will.
  So, don't worry about the people from your past,
  There's a reason why they didn't make it to your future.
  Give flowers to everyone you don't want to lose this year.
  - From the Beauty Solon in the "Hood"

- Mala yerba nunca muere! Bad grass (weeds) never dies!
  - Dennise Carignan, Panama and US

- If you have money and establish a relationship with someone with no money, then prepare to share.
  - Frederick Jordan

- You, who are without sin, throw the first stone.
  - Jesus Christ

- If your heart is not in it, why keep me hanging on? Tell me now and I'll be gone.
  - Singer and Writer

- When people treat you like they don't care, BELIEVE THEM.
  - Sharon Haynes, Fresno, CA

- An angel wrote: Many people will walk in and out of your life, but only true friends will leave footprints in your heart. (Others will leave a footprint on your a__).
  - *From the "Hood"*

ON RELIGION - *Quotes*

- "I AM TOO BLESSED TO BE STRESSED!" The shortest distance between a problem and a solution is the distance between your knees and the floor.
  - *From the Church in the "Hood"*

- God didn't promise days without pain,
  Laughter without sorrow,
  Sun without rain….
  But he did promise strength for the day,
  Comfort for the tears,
  And light for the way.
  - *From the Church in the "Hood"*

- If God brings you to it, He will bring you through it
  - *From the Church in the "Hood"*

- Whenever I am tempted, whenever clouds arise,
  When songs give place to sighing, when hope within me dies,
  I draw closer to Him, from care He sets me free,
  His eye is on the sparrow, and I know He watches me.
  His eye is on the sparrow, and I know He watches me.

I sing because I'm happy, I sing because I'm free,
For His eye is on the sparrow, and I know He watches me.
- *Words by Civilla D. Martin 1905. Inspired by Matthew 10:29-31*

- The will of God will never take you where the Grace of God will not protect you.
  - *From the Church in the "Hood"*

- When God takes something from your grasp, He is not punishing you, but merely opening your hands to receive something better.
  - *From the Church in the "Hood"*

ON RELIGION - *Jokes*

- One evening the Devil was driving down the road and ran out of gas. His car happened to stop right in front of a little Baptist Church having evening prayer revival. When he walked into the door for help, the Preacher saw him first, and jumped out of a large window behind the pulpit. The congregation turned, saw the devil, and jumped out the window also. However, one elderly lady could not negotiate the window and she turned to the approaching devil and said, "Mr. Devil, I have been a Christian all my life. I have not missed an evening revival prayer meeting in 35 years. But, Mr. Devil, I want you to know that I am on your side."
  - *Frederick Jordan, Author, The Lynching of the American Dream*

ON SEX - *Quotes*

- The most important sex organ is the brain.

ON SEX - *Story*

- A man lies dying of unknown causes and says to his wife at his bedside, "My wife, you have been faithful to me over the years. Now I must make some confessions to you in my last hour of life." His wife pleaded with him that any confessions were not necessary and to keep those matters between him and his God. "My wife," he insisted, "I have to confess that I had sex with your best girl friend. I also had sex with your sister and your co-worker." In a disturbed manner, she drew closer and responded, "I knew that. Now I have a confession to make: that's why I put the poison in your food."
  - Andre Jordan, Washington, D. C.

ON SHOPPING - *Quotes*

- I don't buy my potatoes from the gas station.
  - From the "Hood"

ON SHOPPING - *Story*

- A homeowner was looking for life insurance for his family and ran across 3 insurance salesmen having lunch. Learning of the homeowner's desires, one salesman proudly offers his policy to cover from:
    "Basket to the Casket"
  The other one promptly put his policy forward to cover from:
    "Womb to the Tomb"
  But the third salesman closed the deal by offering a policy to cover from:
    "Conception to Resurrection"
  - Kevin Bostin, Author, "Smart Money Moves for African Americans"

ON SLAVERY - *Quotes*

- As I would not be a slave, so I would not be a master.
  - Abraham Lincoln, "On Slavery and Democracy," 1865

- I saved hundreds of slaves, and I could have saved more… if they only knew they were slaves.
  - Harriet Tubman, Underground Railroad

- Of all the tyrannies on humankind, the worst is that which persecutes the mind.
  - John Dryden

- We hold these truths to be self-evident: that all men are created equal; that they are endowed by their Creator with certain inalienable rights; that among those are life, liberty, and the pursuit of happiness.
  - Thomas Jefferson (owned 187 slaves), Signer, Declaration of Independence, 4 July 1776

ON STRUGGLE - *Quotes*

- If there is no struggle, there is no progress. Those who profess to favor freedom, and yet depreciate agitation, are men who want crops without plowing up the ground. They want rain without thunder and lightning. They want the ocean without the awful roar of the many waters. The struggle may be a moral one, or it may be a physical one, or it may be both moral and physical, but it must be a struggle.

Power concedes nothing without a demand; it never did, and it never will.
- *Frederick Douglass*

- A man who won't die for something is not fit to live.
  - *Dr. Martin Luther King Jr.*

- The ultimate measure of a man is not where he stands in times of comfort and convenience, but where he stands in times of challenge and controversy.
  - *Dr. Martin Luther King, Jr.*

- Those who pursue justice in earnest are not afraid of the consequences.
  - *Frederick Jordan*

- I would rather die on my feet, than live on my knees!
  - *James Brown, Singer*

- Out of the night that covers me, black as the pit from pole to pole, I thank whatever gods may be, for my unconquerable soul. In the fell clutch of circumstance, I have not winced nor cried aloud. Under the bludgeoning's of chance, my head is bloody, but unbowed. Beyond this place of wrath and tears looms but the horror of the shade,
  And yet the menace of the years, finds and shall find me unafraid. It matters not how strait the gate, how charged with punishments the scroll,
  I am the master of my fate, I am the captain of my soul.
  - *Invictus*

ON STRESS - *Quotes*

- A good way to overcome stress is to help others out of theirs.
  - Dada Waswani, Indian Spiritual Leader

ON SUCCESS - *Quotes*

- If I have seen further than others, it is by standing on the shoulders of giants.
  - Isaac Newton

- Winners never quit!
  Quitters never win.
  - From the "Hood"

- Success in life is measured not only by what you have done, but by how far you have come.
  - Frederick Jordan

ON SUCCESS - *Story*

- The road to success is not straight; there is a curve called FAILURE, a loop called CONFUSION, speed bumps called FINANCE, red lights called PREJUDICE, caution lights called family and friends. You will also have flats called jobs. But if you have a spare called DETERMINATION, an engine called PERSEVERANCE, insurance called FAITH, a driver called JESUS, you will make it to a place called SUCCESS.
  - Frederick Jordan

ON SURVIVAL - *Quotes*

- It's a mighty poor rat that has only one hole to crawl in.
  - *From the "Hood"*

- To survive, I have had to lie, cheat, and steal…. I've had to "steal" every opportunity denied to me as a Black man. I have had to "cheat" incarceration, sickness, and death. And, to make it through the night, I've had to "lie" with the one I love.
  - *US Congressman Danny K. Davis, Southside, Chicago*

- When life gets stormy,
  And the seas get wavy,
  Ya gotta be like a ship in the Navy,
  Knowing it's going to stay afloat,
  Because it's a boat.
  - *From the "Hood"*

ON SURVIVAL - *Jokes*

- A plane was having problems and losing altitude. The captain came on the audio system and said, "Ladies and gentlemen, we have dumped all of the cargo and continue to lose altitude. We will need some of you to sacrifice your lives so that the rest of us can make it to the next airport. The best way to do this is to call on groups alphabetically."

  "The first group-African Americans," he continued. Several people stood up, went to the door, and jumped. A little boy stood up and his father said, "Sit down, Son." With the plane still losing altitude, the next call was for "Black people."

Several other people jumped, and the same little boy stood up and his father told him to sit down. The third call was for "colored people" and the father told his son to sit down again. Puzzled, the little boy asked, "If we are not African-American, Black, or Colored, then what are we?" The father responded, "Today, we are Negroes."
- *Frederick Jordan*

ON TEAMWORK - *Story*

- A guy was driving down the road and ran into a ditch. He noticed a mule in the adjacent field and asked the father if his mule could pull his car out. After hitching, he blindfolded the mule. Then he commanded, "Git up, Toby," and the mule just stood there. Then he shouted, "Git up, Buster," but the mule just stood there. Then he cried, "Git up, Dusty," and the mule gently pulled the car out of the ditch. The car's owner asked, "Why did you call the other names when the mule's name was Dusty?" The farmer replied, "If Dusty thought he was the only one working, he would never pull that car out of the ditch."
  - *Unknown*

- On November 2002, the Oakland Raiders won over the New England Patriots. Oakland's quarterback, Ken Stabler, threw a near perfect 24 of 28 pass completions, with Jerry Rice catching many of them. Next morning, the popular former Raider Coach John Madden commented, to the amazement of the KCBS Radio staff, on how outstanding the offensive pass defense was. After 5 minutes, he gave recognition to Stabler and Rice. Teamwork!
  - *Frederick Jordan*

ON THIRD WORLD - *Story (Corruption)*

- A third-world country wanted its own national airline and could only afford to buy one plane. A highly qualified American pilot, with 25 years of commercial flying experience, was the first to be interviewed as the pilot. His requested salary was $5,000 a month. The second person interviewed was a European, with seven years experience, who requested $3,500 a month. The third person, with no experience, walked into the room, sat down, put his feet up on the desk, and stated he would guarantee the best service. After the questioning of his experience, which was none, he gave a price for his service of $7,000 a month. The interview panel was amazed and asked him to explain. His response:$1,000 for you, $1,000 for me, and we will go get that American to fly the plane. He got the job!
  - *Unknown*

ON TIME - *Quotes*

- The Present....
  Yesterday is history,
  Tomorrow a mystery,
  Today is a gift!
  That's why it's called the "present."
  We must live the fullness of every moment.
  - *Frederick Jordan*

- A Minute...
  I have only just a minute
  Only sixty seconds in it.

Forced upon me, can't refuse it,
Didn't seek it, didn't choose it,
But it's up to me to use it.

I must suffer if I lose it,
Give account if I abuse it.

Just a tiny little minute
But eternity is in it.
- *Tavis Smiley quoting a noted African American, San Francisco*

ON UNITY - *Quotes*

- Unity is the most powerful force in the universe.
  - *Danny K. Davis, US Congressman, Chicago 10/27/02*

ON WAR - *Quotes*

- To contemplate war is to think about the most horrible of human experiences. On this February day, as this nation stands at the brink of battle (Iraq), every American on some level must be contemplating the horrors of war.
  - *Senate Floor Speech by US Senator Robert Bird, Feb. 12, 2003*

- Old men make war for young men to fight.
  - *From the "Hood"*

ON WAR - *Joke*

- In the 1800's, there was a Buffalo Soldier stationed at the Presidio in San Francisco who was very effective at fighting the Indians and protecting the frontier. One day he found himself surrounded by Indians and the Chief rode in and stated, "We heard about you and your horse, Mr. Buffalo man. However, you have protected the white man against our people and therefore you must die. But I will give you three wishes."

The Buffalo Soldier said, "Bring me my horse, Buster." The soldier whispered in the horse's ear and the horse took off over the hill and returned with a beautiful blonde. The Chief said, "That's a smart horse," and offered his tepee. After the horse took the blonde back, the soldier asked for his horse on his second wish. This time Buster returned with a bosomed redhead. The Chief said, "Now that's a smart horse," and offered his tepee again, reminding him he had only one more wish. Again, the soldier asked for his horse and pleaded, "Buster, for the last time I want you to read my lips! I said, bring posse, posse!"
- *Unknown*

ON WEALTH - *Quotes*

- My children are not rich. I am! They need to make their own money in life.
  - *Shaquille O'Neal, Professional Basketball Player*

- God bless the child that got his own.
  - *Your Mother*

ON WINNING - *Quotes*

- Push yourself again and again. Don't give an inch until the final buzzer sounds.
  - Larry Bird, Professional Basketball Player, Boston Celtics

- If you don't have confidence, you will always find a way not to win.
  - Carl Lewis, U. S. Track and Field, nine Olympic Gold Medals

- I was built this way for a reason, so I'm going to use it.
  - Simone Biles, U. S. Gymnastics, 32 Olympic and World Championship medals, most decorated gymnast of all time

ON WORK - *Quotes*

- My work has me busier than a one-legged man in an "ass-kicking contest."
  - Andre Jordan, former Dep. Chief of US Federal Agency

- If you love your job, then you will never have to work a day in your life.
  - Frederick Jordan

QUOTES, JOKES AND STORIES TO LIVE BY

INDEX

(WHAT DID THEY SAY)

A

Abraham Lincoln, President of US during Civil War/End of Slavery pg. 16

Albert Einstein's Teacher pg. 16

Alexander Graham Bell, Inventor, Scientist and Engineer pg. 33

Alice Cooper, American Writer pg. 34

Angela Davis, Political Activist, Author, Professor UC Santa Cruz pg. 35

Angelina Jolie, Actress, Filmmaker, one of highest paid actresses pg. 41

Andre Jordan, Former Deputy Chief, United States Park Police pg. 38, 45 & 54

Antoine de Saint-Exupery, French Aviator, Author and Poet pg. 29

Archbishop Desmond Tutu, Anti-apartheid Activist, Nobel Prize pg. 16

Aretha Franklin, American Singer, Songwriter, Pianist pg. 29

B

Barack Obama, 44th President of the United States pg. 37
Bill Jones, KBLX Radio Station DJ pg. 26
Bobby Womack, American Singer, Musician and Songwriter pg. 11

D

(14th) Dalai Lama, highest Spiritual Leader of Tibet pg. 25
Dale Dawson, College Professor pg. 16
Danny K. Davis, US Congressman, Illinois pg. 52
Deepak Chopra, Author pg. 34
Dennise Carignan, San Francisco Carnaval Organizer pg. 42
Dr. Mae Jamison, Engineer, Physician, former Nasa Astronaut pg. 25
Dr. Mera Horne, D. Sc., Mechanical Engineer, NASA pg. 41
Danny K. Davis, US Congressman, Illinois pg. 52

E

Elena Restituyo, Special Education Teacher pg. 23

F

Frank Devlin, Construction Manager of Projects pg. 19
Frank Outlaw, "Inspirational Quotes" and American Businessman pg. 17
Frederick Douglas, Abolitionist, Writer, Advisor-US Pres. Lincoln pg. 38

G

General Sen Tsu, "The Art of War" pg. 17
George Bernard Shaw, Irish playwright, critic and Political Activist pg. 10
George Fraser, Author/Inspirational Speaker pg. 21
George Santayana, Spanish-American Philosopher pg. 17

H

Harriet Tubman, Operated the Underground Railroad for Slaves pg. 22

I

Isaac Newton, Mathematician, Physicist, Astronomer pg. 48

J

Jack McKnight, Interior Designer and Businessman pg. 9
James Brown, American Singer/Musician, "Godfather of Soul" pg. 47
Jan Murray, Stand-up Comedian, Actor and Game Show Host pg. 31
Jesus Christ, Religious Leader and Central figure of Christianity pg. 42
John Dryden, 17th century English Poet and Playwright pg. 46
John Frederick, Maryland Farmer and Fred Jordan's Grandfather pg. 22
John Tolson, Interior Designer and Contractor pg. 22
Joseph Oakley, Civil and Structural Engineer Consultant pg. 19
Julius Maada Bio, President of Sierra Leone since 2018 pg. 18

K

Kwame Nkrumah, First President of Ghana pg. 23

L

Larry Ivory, Board Chair, National Black Chamber of Commerce pg. 11
Lewis Jordan, Businessman, and Fred Jordan's Father pg. 25
Lyndon Baines Johnson, 36th President of United States pg. 23

M

Malcolm X, Black Muslim, Civil Rights Activist pg. 18
Maria Lourdes Cuaresma, Accounting Executive pg. 30
Marcus Garvey, Pan-Africanist and Political Activist pg. 22
Marion Berry, former Mayor of the District of Columbia pg. 41

N

Nannette Cutliff, Chief Financial Officer, Walnut Creek, CA pg. 7
Neville Brothers, Soul and Jazz Group, New Orleans pg. 38
Nur Abby Hussein, Challenger for President of Somaliland pg. 25

R

Reinhold Niebubr, Theologian, ethicist and political analyst pg. 38
Richard Harding, Journalist and Writer pg. 34
Robert Kennedy, US Attorney General, Advisor Pres Kennedy pg.35

S

Samuel Johnson, English Critic, Biographer, Poet of 18th century pg. 34
Satchel Paige, Oldest Professional Baseball player pg. 9
Shaquille O'Neal, Former basketball player ad Sports analyst pg. 53
Sharon Blanco, Real Estate Manager pg. 17
Sharon Haynes, Gourmet Dessert Business pg. 42
Sherry Patton, Gourmet Cook pg. 37
Simone Biles, The most decorated gymnast in history pg. 41

T

Timothy Simon, Lawyer and former CA PUC Commissioner pg. 35
Thomas Cronin, Political Scientist and Academic Administrator pg. 27

W

Warren Buffett, business, Investor, Billionaire and Philanthropist pg. 10
Winston Churchill, Prime Minister, United Kingdom, World War II pg. 39
Wolfgang Amadeus Davis, Journalist and Writer pg. 34
Wynn Davis, Author, The Best of Success pg. 7

Y

Yolanda Woodard, Los Angeles Entrepreneur, Political Activist pg. 37

Z

Zip Ziglar, American Artist pg. 14

NOTE TO MY READERS

If you have enjoyed reading my book and found worthy advice for the challenges or quality of life you seek, then why not refer this book to your friends and family to purchase at Amazon, Barnes & Noble, etc. Also, if you have a favorite quote, joke or story that you live by, email it to me with permission to use your name or remain anonymous for possible inclusion in my next edition? My email address is <u>frederickjordan308@gmail.com</u>.

Sincerely,
Frederick Jordan, Author

"ON POWER OF MIND" (Children)

This dog running through the forest came across this huge bone and stopped to enjoy it. Meanwhile a Jaguar saw the dog and was slipping up on the dog for a quick meal of the dog. The dog sees the Jaguar easing up on him and says in a loud voice, "Boy, that was a good Jaguar, I wonder where I could find another Jaguar with bones like that?" The Jaguar hears this and turns around to run away. But there was a monkey in the tree watching the whole thing with the dog having the bone, jealously catches up with the Jaguar and tells him the whole story. The angry Jaguar turns back for the dog with the monkey on his back. The dog again, pretending that he doesn't see them coming, says in a real loud voice, "I wonder where that monkey is that was to bring me another Jaguar. The Jaguar, hearing this, stops in its track, turns around, eats the monkey and runs off into the forest.

There was a frog by the stream complaining about the administration of the jungle by the Lion. The Lion hears about the complaints and shows up at the stream watering hole and calls all the animals around. "Someone here is not happy with me being the King of the Jungle and he knows who he is" growls the Lion. the Lion continued, "he lives in the water and on land and has a big mouth!" The frog knew that would be the end of him and quickly jumps up on the rock in front of all the animals and shouts, "let's go kill that crocodile!"

—*Elena Restituyo, Special Education Teacher,*
San Francisco and La Veda, Dominican Republic

www.ingramcontent.com/pod-product-compliance
Lightning Source LLC
LaVergne TN
LVHW052004060526
838201LV00059B/3834